Sierra

SPIRIT
of the CIMARRON

Sierra

by KATHLEEN DUEY

DreamWorks®

TM & © 2002 DreamWorks LLC

Text by Kathleen Duey

Published in the United States 2002 by Dutton Children's Books,

a division of Penguin Putnam Books for Young Readers

345 Hudson Street, New York, New York 10014

www.penguinputnam.com

Printed in USA First Edition

ISBN: 0-525-46712-2

1 3 5 7 9 10 8 6 4 2

The characters and story in this book were inspired by the
DreamWorks film *Spirit: Stallion of the Cimarron*.

Chapter One

Bonita, my mother, has a coat as white as snow. When I was a foal, I loved that I could always spot her in the herd, even in the darkest night. The year I left her forever, spring came fast. The weather turned so suddenly that the creeks overflowed with snowmelt. The wildflowers were thick and sweet. We came onto the prairie from our canyon winter-grounds. The sky seemed wider than it ever had. I was restless. As we traveled slowly toward the foothills, I was always in trouble with Tally.

Sierra danced around Paco. The old burro tipped his long ears back and stared at her. Sierra had known him all her life and she understood him perfectly. She shook her mane.

Paco did not gallop and jump for fun. Not anymore. It was warm out, his belly was full of new grass and he wanted to nap, not play. He wanted her to go away and leave him alone.

Sierra galloped off, kicking her heels skyward, then slowed to prance past her mother.

Bonita's white coat was shining in the sun. She was dozing next to Shadow, the herd's stallion. Tally, the lead mare, stood near them. Like all the rest of them, Bonita didn't bother to open her eyes at the sound of Sierra's hoofbeats.

Sierra knew why.

She had been galloping and playing all morning and the older horses, including her mother, were tired of her disturbing them—just like Paco was.

Sierra tossed her head. Only the early foals, stilting along on their unsteady legs, seemed as silly with spring as she was—but they were no fun to gallop with. They were too clumsy, and she had to be really careful not to hurt them.

Sierra slowed to a trot and cast a look at Fern, the only other filly in the herd about her age. They had played together all of their lives. Sierra was faster, but not by much.

There was no use trying to rouse Fern into a race this morning, though. The gangly sorrel mare was lying down and sound asleep in the shade of a cottonwood tree.

Sierra shook her mane restlessly, then broke into a canter. She ran in a long circle around the herd, jumping a fallen tree and landing neatly in a clump of lacy ferns without breaking her stride. She raced through the wildflowers, startling bees into the air, ducking her head to smell the blooms as she went.

Then, turning a long, gradual arc at the far end of the meadow, Sierra started back toward the herd. The horses were scattered across the hillside, most of them dozing with their heads low, hips slanted, one back hoof tipped up.

Sierra cantered past a group of mares who stood

muzzle-to-tail, grooming each other's backs. Not one looked up at her. Their foals danced a little as Sierra passed, but none tried to chase her. She was glad.

She didn't want to have to stop to lead a wayward foal back to its mother. Sierra knew that Tally would never forgive her if her springtime foolishness hurt a foal.

Sierra cantered close to Paco again. He tossed his head and switched his tail disapprovingly. Her hooves clattering on a stony patch of ground, Sierra passed Fern so closely that the young mare was startled awake and scrambled to her feet.

Sierra tossed her head and angled her direction in order to see.

Good!

Fern was chasing her.

Sierra veered off and started uphill, her strides bunching into leaping bounds as the slope steepened. She could hear Fern's hooves on the ground behind her and slowed just enough to let the young sorrel mare catch up easily.

The instant that Fern was beside her, Sierra

leaned into a hard turn, bolting ahead and veering across the slope. She stretched out, pounding along a deer trail that led through the pines, letting her hooves fly and flash. Fern galloped along, just behind her.

Sierra galloped through the sun-dappled shade of a tall cottonwood. Fern stayed close behind her, her nostrils flared as she worked to keep up. They pretended to be frightened, as though they were running from wolves—not simply enjoying a morning gallop.

Sierra turned again, leading Fern nearly straight up the slope. They both tried to get ahead, bounding almost in unison. Winded as they topped the ridge, Sierra broke back into a trot, glancing at the herd below. Fern slowed, too, her sides heaving from the long run.

Sierra stared. From up here the horses looked small, unfamiliar. She could pick out her mother easily, and Shadow, and Paco—and all the rest if she tried. But if she didn't try, she could pretend that she had nothing to do with them, that she was all alone. On an impulse, she turned to look away from the herd and stood staring at the woods that stretched as far as she could see.

What would it be like to be alone?

Sierra shivered the skin on her back. Fern tilted her head and straightened her ears, curious about Sierra's sudden uneasiness. Sierra shook her mane to get rid of the odd feeling and looked down at the familiar herd.

She knew them all.

And of course they were there, close by, in case of trouble.

Fern made a sudden whuffling sound deep in her throat.

Sierra glanced at her.

The tall sorrel mare was standing rigidly, her ears pointed at a thicket a few strides away. Sierra stared and went still, lifting her head. She listened.

There.

It was a faint rustling sound, but there was something about it that let Sierra know instantly that it was not a mouse or a covey of quail, or anything *small*.

Fern fidgeted. Sierra arched her neck. She felt her own hooves getting skittishly light on the earth as she stared at the thicket.

Another spate of rustling erupted. Sierra strained to see. It sounded like something huge, like a wolf or a lion.

Fern's eyes were rimmed in white. She struck a hoof against the ground and Sierra felt her own courage rise. If it was a wolf, if they stuck together, they could run it off. But what if it was *two* wolves?

Abruptly, the leaves parted just enough to show the face of a deer. Her gentle brown eyes were open wide and her surprise at seeing the two fillies standing stiffly in front of her was obvious.

Sierra ducked her muzzle and pretended to be rubbing her foreleg. She twitched her tail and glanced sideways. Fern was gazing casually out across the countryside, then looking back as though she had just noticed the doe.

Once the doe was in the open and had looked around, she turned, looking back along her own flank at the thicket. Silently, a fawn appeared, its coat dappled with white like sunlight through leaves. A few seconds later a second fawn stepped out of the leaves, a little smaller than the first, but shiny-coated and healthy looking.

Sierra blinked, then exchanged a look with Fern. Twins!

Sierra stared at the babies. A quick stamp of the doe's cloven hoof reminded Sierra of her manners.

She turned aside just enough to be polite, and watched the fawns from the corner of her eye as their mother picked her way past and started down the slope.

The fawns were beautiful, their big ears swiveling this way and that as they went.

Sierra blew out a long breath. Fern reached out to nudge her shoulder and Sierra blinked, still looking at the deer. She knew what Fern wanted, of course. The idea of facing danger without Shadow and the others nearby to help fight had made her nervous. She wanted to go back to the herd.

Sierra switched her tail. Her own heart was racing and she still felt uneasy. What if the deer had been a bear, angered at being disturbed? Or a pack of wolves?

Still, Sierra hesitated. She wheeled around to look downhill. Her mother's white coat stood out like a full moon at night. Fern nudged Sierra's shoulder again and she gave in. They started back together. Sierra let Fern lead the way.

Chapter Two

*W*e saw humans from a distance one morning, at a watering hole. We could hear their odd voices clearly on the still air. They were leading horses and we stared as we always did when we saw horses with them. We stayed well hidden, of course. The humans left behind their odd scent, part smoke and part stink.

It was hot early that year. The flowers curled into brittle spirals. We longed for rain. When it finally came, it made me even more foolish than usual—and this time it caused terrible trouble.

The summer warmed. The days got longer, and hotter. The horses moved toward the foothills where the creek bottoms still held grass.

Sierra usually woke before the others and waited silently for the sunrise. As the horses around her woke, they all stood listening to the quail's morning calls, the rustling of the night creatures returning home. Then, as the first rays of the sun fanned out over the land, the herd set about the work of finding food and water for the day.

Tally always set off first, with Bonita next, and the rest following. Shadow brought up the rear. His head was always up, his battle-scarred ears flicking back and forth, his nostrils flared. He searched for danger in every stone, every clump of sage, every breath of air.

This morning, Tally led them to a section of creek bottom filled with grass. Sierra cantered around the herd, coaxing Fern into running with her at first. Then she went on alone.

Once she had run enough to settle her spirits, Sierra quieted and set about grazing, snatching up huge mouthfuls of the grass, staying close to Fern.

As the sun sailed higher and brighter, Sierra kept glancing at Tally. When the lead mare finally tossed her head and began to walk, Sierra was grateful. It was time to find shade.

The horses all walked slowly, sleepy from a morning of good grazing and creek water.

Sierra knew that if it was up to her mother, they would go to the ridge. Tally sometimes let Bonita lead the way. Other times, Tally stubbornly led them down the dry creek bed or back across the washout gully to a stand of cottonwoods that stood in the center of a flat plain. Today, as hot as it was, Sierra was hoping for the ridge. There would be more breeze up high.

Sierra glanced back at Shadow, ambling along behind the herd. His head was high, and beside him was old Paco, jogging to keep up with the horses' longer strides.

Paco and Shadow were friends, Sierra knew. She had never seen Shadow fight with the brave little burro. And Paco had always helped watch for danger.

Shadow was alert, but relaxed. He trusted Tally and Bonita and he nearly always let his mares figure out which copse of cottonwood trees or creek-bottom willow seemed best each day.

The day was getting warmer. The sun seemed to get hotter with every step Sierra took. She walked with her head down, half dozing as they went.

Sierra bumped into Fern when the horses stopped. Lifting her head, she stepped aside to see over the backs of the mares in front of her.

Her mother and Tally were standing on a deer trail, heads lowered, blowing up puffs of dust with their breath. Then they stood side by side with their heads up, their dusty upper lips curled back so that they could scent the trail grit clinging to their muzzles.

Sierra blew out a long breath, then stamped one back hoof against the baked earth. Now they would all have to stand in the sun until Tally and Bonita went on. If they delayed too long, Shadow might come up to see what was the matter. But he rarely did that. He rarely had to.

Tally and Bonita almost never disagreed. When they did, Tally usually won out. She was bigger, and she had been part of the herd when Sierra's mother had joined it. Tally didn't need Shadow's support to win arguments.

A three-year-old colt behind Sierra stamped a forehoof and shook his head. Out of the corner of her eye, Sierra saw him arching his neck and sidling impatiently. Then he reached out to nip at the mare in front of him, as though he wanted to overrule the lead mare's decision and move on.

Sierra looked over her shoulder. Shadow was staring at the colt. It wouldn't be long before Shadow made him leave the herd, Sierra knew—probably next spring.

It was always that way. The young stallion would band with other young stallions until he could win his own herd of mares. They were safe enough, ranging together, and because there would be no colts among them, they wouldn't attract wolves or mountain lions' attention.

Sierra stared straight ahead, wishing Tally and

her mother would hurry. At last, Tally snorted and shook her head. Then she moved on. Sierra followed with the others. When she crossed the deer trail she caught a faint scent that made her shiver. Wolves?

Sierra exchanged a glance with Fern as they followed Tally uphill toward the ridge. It was summer—they shouldn't have to worry about wolves now. Sierra pulled in a slow breath. The scent was mixed with the dry dust of the trail. It was old. It had to be.

Wolves rarely came out of the mountains in the summer. Why would they? The foals and fawns were fleet and swift by now, no longer easy prey. The jackrabbits and mice the wolves usually hunted were more plentiful high in the foothills this time of year.

Tally set such a lazy pace that by the time she stopped to peer into the shade beneath the cottonwoods, Sierra's back felt afire from the sun's heat. Sierra shivered her skin and switched her tail, wishing Tally would hurry, but knowing she would not.

Tally was cautious. So was Bonita. They spent a long time staring into the shadows and scenting the wind.

Sierra stood watching larks dart among the branches, dragonflies looping among the trunks. Everything seemed normal. There was no trace of wolf scent, no flicker of wolf tail or a flash of yellowish wolf eye here. Why did they have to wait?

Shadow finally came forward and Sierra wondered if the old wolf-scent on the deer trail had made him as uneasy as it had Tally and her mother. The sun battered the horses from above, but none of them dared to press forward, not until Tally and Shadow stopped staring and started walking.

When Shadow approached the trees alone, his head up and his nostrils flaring, Sierra felt herself tense. But Shadow nickered softly and Tally went on. The rest of the horses came forward at a trot, eager to be out of the sun.

Sierra felt the shadows ease the heat of her skin the instant she passed into the shade. All around her the horses were blowing out deep breaths of relief. Sierra and Fern found a place a little apart from the others and stood close, both of them swishing their tails to shoo each other's flies.

Grateful to be out of the worst of the heat, Sierra stood with her head low, letting time flow past, waiting for the evening to come. Fern closed her eyes and after a time, Sierra let herself doze, too. Shadow would stand vigil. He always did.

It was a sudden hot breeze fluttering the cottonwood leaves that woke Sierra. She opened her eyes to find Fern already awake, staring out from beneath the trees at the arch of the prairie sky. While they slept, the day had changed completely.

A storm was rushing across the prairie. The blue sky was darkening fast and Sierra heard the rumble of distant thunder. The very air felt alive. Sierra rippled her skin, shifting her weight. Fern tossed her head.

The mares with little foals were seeking the densest cottonwoods. If rain came, they would take whatever shelter they could find. The young mares shuffled uneasily while the older ones stood quietly, waiting with their ears up.

Shadow paced in a circle around them all, his step quick and certain. Lightning flickered. A false dusk settled over the land. Thunder rumbled again, closer. A second later, there was another flicker of light. Sierra shied a little at the booming sound. It was getting closer.

Sierra tossed her head and shook her mane, then walked a few steps, her head high, facing the wind. Fern joined her, her eyes wide enough to be rimmed in white. The storm roared toward them.

Impulsively, Sierra leaped into a canter, galloping in a short curve down the slope, crossing the deer trail in a single bound, then coming back toward the herd. She passed so close to Fern that the young sorrel mare had to leap aside.

Sierra glanced backward. Perfect! It had worked, as usual. Fern was galloping now, too, stretching out to catch up with her friend. Sierra galloped happily beneath the next veined arch of lightning, bracing herself for the crashing rumble that followed it.

The first spatter of rain was light, driven and lifted by the wind. Sierra felt the fat drops of water seep through her coat and touch her skin. She whinnied for sheer joy. The heat was gone, gone, gone. The oppressive sleepy day was now exciting, an excuse for a joyful gallop.

Sierra looked back toward the stand of trees. The rest of the herd was staying closer, a few of the younger mares dancing and cantering in tight circles. The foals were playing, their long, silly legs a flashing tangle as they reared and kicked.

Sierra could see her mother's white coat, standing out against the gloom of the storm. She could see Tally, too, and Shadow. It was a joy to gallop wildly like this and still be close enough to the herd to feel safe. Curving in a long sweeping turn, Sierra started back toward the herd, then veered to jump a clump of sage. Fern kept up. She kicked her heels high, and Sierra responded with a back-arching leap, pawing once at the sky before she went on, catching her stride again.

The rain thickened, and Sierra felt it coursing

down her sides, cooling her until she shivered with excitement. The thunder shook the ground and Sierra bolted from a gallop into a mad run that flew her over the ground.

Fern labored to keep up, but couldn't. Sierra was lost in a feeling of glory in her own strength and the fierce pounding of the rain on her back. Lightning sparkled overhead. The thunder that followed it seemed to run through the soil, not the sky.

Sierra veered again, this time to leap a narrow creek. She heard Fern behind her, her breathing quick and her hoofbeats a-clatter on the stony soil. The scent of wet brush filled the air, erasing the usual smells of dust and deer and rabbits.

Sierra gathered herself to jump a clump of sage, tucking her forelegs perfectly. The leaves brushed her belly as she went over, landing in perfect rhythm, her stride beginning again a single beat after it had left off.

Glorying in the wild, watery smell of the storm, Sierra leaned into another long curve, but a low bluff cut her off. She recognized it—she had gotten farther from the herd than she had meant to. Behind her, Fern was coming up hard, swerving to one side to keep from running into her.

It was in that instant that Sierra saw the wolves.

A blend of rain gray and earth brown, they were nearly invisible in the downpour that had hidden even their strong, musky scent.

Sierra squealed and slid to a stop, wrenching around. She saw the astonishment in Fern's eyes and the flicker of fear, then Fern managed to turn. They raced away together, the wolves at their heels.

Sierra galloped without thinking, terror shoving her along, headed straight back to the stand of cottonwoods. Fern's fear made her faster than she had ever been and she stayed abreast as they fled, charging up the ridge together, the wolves snapping at them, snarling low in their throats.

Sierra heard Shadow's scream of rage, then saw him flash past as she and Fern skittered to a sliding, plunging stop among the mares.

Shadow reared, striking out at the biggest of the

wolves. It dodged deftly, fading to one side. Shadow wheeled around and reared again, springing forward on his hind legs, baring his teeth. The wolf retreated, spinning around to run a few steps, then facing Shadow again.

That was when Sierra noticed the other wolves, silent and slinking, as they closed a circle around Shadow. Paco brayed, loud and long, the grating rasp of his voice startling everyone, including the wolves, as he charged forward.

Shadow plunged to one side, but he didn't let the smaller wolves distract him. While Paco struck out at two of them, Shadow lunged straight at the wolf leader, his head low and his teeth slashing.

The leader squealed and jumped backward, but several smaller ones dashed closer, snapping at Shadow's back legs as he backed up for another charge. Shadow's scream of pain was terrible and Sierra felt it pierce her heart.

Paco had run off the two young wolves, but he whirled around when Shadow screamed and focused on another one. Just behind the brave burro came

Tally, then two of the younger stallions, neighing and galloping with flattened ears as they drove the wolves away from Shadow.

Bonita charged forward and some of the other mares followed her. Snarling, the wolves finally scattered, fading back into the rain, leaving only their sharp scent behind.

Sierra shivered as the horses settled, Shadow limping to stand among his herd, Paco close beside him. The rain kept falling and as the night stormed around them, even the hated scent of the wolves dimmed and washed away.

Chapter Three

I knew I had made a terrible mistake. But the rain had washed away the wolf scent or I never would have run right into the pack like that. But whether I meant to or not, my wild gallop had very nearly cost Shadow his life. What happened afterward was terrible for me, too. I know it was even worse for Fern. It changed her forever. It changed, me, too, but differently.

The sun rose the next morning on a soaked and sparkling earth. After the long night of lightning

24

and fear, Sierra welcomed the light gratefully. The earth was wet, balling up inside her hooves as she walked, slippery when she headed downslope to nip a mouthful of grass. She kept glancing up at the herd, watching Shadow.

Sierra blinked as Shadow moved around a group of mares. His wound had stiffened and he could barely walk. Sierra felt terrible. Her foolishness had caused this. Then, just behind the foolishness, she felt fear.

If Shadow was hurt, they had no real defense against wolves or anything else. Sierra stopped grazing and started back toward the herd, her uneasiness guiding her instinctively toward her mother.

Tally suddenly moved to block her way. Sierra stopped, confused. Tally came forward, her head high, forcing Sierra to back up, sliding a little in the mud.

Sierra waited, expecting at least one sharp nip. What she had done had endangered them all. She knew that. She lowered her head like an apologetic foal so that Tally could see how sorry she was.

It made no difference. Tally came forward again, her head up. She shouldered Sierra to one side, then circled, and came at her again.

Sierra backed up, then tried to step aside. Tally wouldn't let her. She rolled back on her hindquarters and spun so fast that Sierra could only back up again, her path blocked by Tally's quick move.

Sierra spotted her mother, but Bonita was not facing her. She was studying the hills in the distance, or acting like that was what she was doing. Sierra whickered at her mother. That seemed to anger Tally even more.

Surprised and confused by the rough treatment, Sierra wheeled around and cantered a few strides, sliding to a muddy halt, stopping to look back at Tally. The lead mare wasn't satisfied. She walked toward Sierra, her step heavy and purposeful.

Sierra wheeled around again, feeling her heart thudding hard. She looked upslope at her mother, but Bonita still wasn't watching. Tally forced Sierra back twice more. Then she turned away, starting back toward the herd.

Sierra stood uncertainly. A moment later, Tally

was on her way back down, this time shoving Fern along ahead of her. Fern walked as though she was sick, her head down, her hooves shuffling.

Sierra stood, astonished, as Fern came to stand beside her. They stood shoulder to shoulder as Tally turned away and walked slowly up the rise to the ridge top.

Sierra stared. The herd was waking up, getting ready to move. Shadow was limping badly, but he took his place behind the herd anyway. Sierra saw her mother glance back once, and her heart rose.

But Bonita didn't meet her eyes. She seemed not to know or care that Sierra and Fern were alone at the base of the slope. Bonita just shook her mane and stretched out her neck, waking up. Then she faced forward. Sierra felt terrible. Her mother was as furious with her as Tally was.

Without a single backward look, Tally led off. The rest of the herd strung out in a long line, walking in twos and threes as they always did. The oldest and biggest mares went first, Bonita leading them. Then came the younger mares, mixed with the young stallions, then the mares with foals, the babies playing in circles around them, unused to such a slow pace.

Sierra glanced at Fern. Her head was still down, her ears flattened and her eyes full of misery. She let out a long breath and lowered her head until her muzzle nearly brushed the ground.

Sierra watched the last of the mares disappear from sight, headed down the far side of the bluff. She could see her mother's white coat, standing out from the others as the herd disappeared. Bonita did not look back.

The world around Sierra was suddenly just an empty stretch of sagebrush, no sign that the herd was anywhere close. She felt fear course through her legs. She lifted her head and whinnied, unable to stop herself. She had never in her life been alone like this—been forced to stand apart from the herd she'd been born into. She raised her head and whinnied a second time, calling desperately.

There was no answer.

If her mother had heard, she didn't care how alone Sierra felt. None of them did. And Sierra knew there was no use in galloping to catch up.

Tally wouldn't allow them to join the herd—at least not yet.

Sierra shook herself, glancing around. Was there still a faint scent of wolves in the air? Fern looked terrified. Was it because of the wolves? Were they close? Sierra reached out to touch Fern's shoulder with her muzzle.

Fern stepped backward, nearly stumbling to avoid the touch. Sierra stared. Fern shook her mane and set off, walking with her head and tail low. Sierra stood rigidly still as Fern walked past her, starting up the ridge after the herd. Then she followed, her heart aching. Fern looked different. Changed. Sierra knew that was her fault, too. Fern never would have galloped so far on her own.

All through the long morning hours, Sierra and Fern walked behind the herd, just close enough to see the others. Shadow's limp was terrible and Tally paced the herd to match his gait. She stopped often and the whole herd stood switching flies while Shadow rested.

The first time Tally stopped, Sierra used the pause to catch up. Fern followed, both of them shuffling along at a trot. Tally saw them coming and bolted, galloping toward them, squealing, her head low and her teeth bared.

Fern scrambled backward as Tally charged them. Sierra stood still, preparing to be scolded and nipped.

What she was not prepared for was Tally wheeling around again and leaving them behind once more. Without so much as a backward look, the older mare returned to the herd and led off again.

None of the other horses looked back at Sierra and Fern. Not even Bonita. They all faced forward, grooming each other when they had to stop, swishing their tails to free each other of the gnats that rose from the wet brush. Sierra and Fern could only watch miserably, from a distance.

As the sun slowly slid up the arched sky, Sierra grew more and more sorry for her recklessness. She hated being bossed and shoved by Tally, but that wasn't what was making her miserable. Following behind the herd all day, she couldn't help watching Shadow. He was really hurt. He was brave about keeping up, but Sierra could see how much walking pained him.

Sierra was so preoccupied with her own unhappiness as she watched Shadow limping that she did not realize at first that they were passing the grazing grounds where they had been feeding nearly every day.

Tally kept going, leading the herd slowly but surely away from the range they had come to know so well. Sierra plodded along, careful not to narrow the distance between herself and the herd. The ground beneath her hooves became drier as they went, the mud drying under the fierce sun.

The afternoon was even longer than the morning had been. Sierra kept hoping that her mother would come back to walk with her, or at least look at her when they were stopped for Shadow to rest his injured leg. But she didn't.

Sierra walked slowly, as miserable as she had ever been in her life. As terrible as it was to watch Shadow struggling to limp fast enough to keep up with Tally's slow pace, it was even worse to see Fern stumbling along with her head so low.

Sierra tried two or three times to touch her old friend, but Fern shrank away each time and Sierra gave up.

Tally finally veered off and the herd fanned out in a swale that was thick with grass. Sierra blew out a breath, glad the punishment was over. She took a cautious step toward the herd, then another. Tally's head jerked up and she glared at Sierra.

Sierra stopped and stood rigidly. After a long moment, she lowered her head and pretended to graze. Tally went back to the business of making sure the mares with foals stayed even closer to the herd than usual.

Sierra stood beside Fern for a long time. She stared at Bonita, waiting. Surely her mother would come back to graze beside her, would at least try to make her feel better. But Bonita grazed with Tally and her friends.

Sierra finally moved off, careful to move *away* from the herd, to graze. But her appetite was buried somewhere beneath her fear and regret and she ended up standing still, watching Shadow limp painfully from one clump of grass to the next.

Chapter Four

*T*he days crawled past. Fern and I were left back, every morning, forced to stay apart all day—even to sleep a little way off from the others. Fern's eyes got duller and sadder every day. When the morning finally came that Tally let us take our places at the back of the long line, Fern raised her head a little. I felt a weight lift from my spirit. I promised myself that I would never bring danger to the herd like that again.

As summer stretched itself out, in the afternoons, huge clouds, dark as dusk, would pile up.

Sometimes they flashed with lightning. When the storms came over, Sierra only tossed her head and cantered in short circles with the rest, staying close. She was careful not to run faster or farther than any of the others, no matter how exciting the lightning and thunder became.

Fern remained Sierra's friend, but she was changed. She walked carefully and rarely galloped—and she kept a watchful eye on Tally all the time.

One morning, as the herd came awake and began to stir, the old feelings of restlessness overcame Sierra. Unable to settle herself, she cantered a little way, then turned, keeping her pace slow and circling tightly so she would come right back to the herd.

As she broke back into a trot, she noticed Tally standing with her head high, glaring at her. Sierra shook her mane and slowed to a walk. She had not forgotten the lesson, nor would she—ever. But sometimes it was very hard not to gallop when she wanted to.

Shadow was ambling toward her, his limp much

lessened, the wound nearly healed. Still, he walked slowly, as he had since the wolf attack, headed for his position toward the rear of the herd. As he passed Sierra, he reached out and touched her muzzle with his own.

Sierra was grateful. She glanced again at Tally and found that the lead mare was still staring at her, her head high, her ears laid back. Sierra shook her mane. If Shadow had forgiven her, why couldn't Tally?

Nervous, and feeling rebellious, Sierra deliberately broke into a slow canter again. She swung in a short arc, loping just three or four strides along the top of the ridge. Then she slowed to a trot and was about to start back when something caught her eye.

On the horizon, she saw a single horse.

Sierra stared, waiting for other horses to become visible. But none did. It wasn't a band of young stallions and it wasn't a herd like the one she lived in. Nor was it a group of young mares somehow separated from their friends and family.

As Sierra watched, the horse threw up its head,

then reared, pawing at the sky. Then it began to gallop, straight toward her.

Sierra stepped back, hiding herself in the sage-brush. It was a stallion, that much was sure. His thick, arched neck was unmistakable even at a distance. He was a dark bay—almost black—and he was tall, too; his stride covered the ground in long leaps.

Sierra blew out a troubled breath. Had he seen her? She didn't think so. But he might have. Maybe he would veer off in another direction and never know the herd was on this side of the ridge.

Sierra watched a few seconds longer, then an impatient whinny from Tally made Sierra canter back, plunging to an awkward stop among the horses that were sorting themselves into the long, informal line they would travel in.

Fern stepped away from the others and waited for Sierra to come close. The line began to move, Tally in the lead and Shadow behind.

Sierra walked with Fern, keeping the same ambling pace as the others. She couldn't help glancing back toward the ridge now and then, but there was no sign of the strange stallion. She hoped that he had gone his own way.

The grass was past its prime. The stems were getting tough and many of the grasses had gone to seed. There were a few kinds that had tiny, painful barbs that hooked in the throat and tongue. The horses would no longer touch them.

Tally moved the herd midmorning, then again midafternoon—finding deep green grass both times. The stems were stiff, but the tops were still good forage.

Sierra walked just fast enough to keep up with the others, mostly staying beside Fern. But her mother came to walk beside her late in the afternoon. When they stopped for the day, Bonita and her friends stayed close.

Tally came to stand with Bonita as she often did, but she lowered her head and laid back her ears when she saw Sierra among her favorite companions.

Bonita shook her mane and eased forward, placing herself between Tally and Sierra. The meaning was clear. She thought her daughter had been punished enough for a mistake that she would not take lightly or forget. Bonita nuzzled her daughter and Sierra lifted her own muzzle to touch her mother's shoulder gratefully.

Tally looked around. Sierra hoped the lead mare could see that not one of the other mares was the least bit tense around her. They all stood close, dozing in the shade.

Finally, Tally blew out a long, noisy breath. Then she took up a position next to Bonita and the two mares began to groom each other. Sierra closed her eyes, relieved.

Two days later, the herd had just begun to move when Tally stopped, her head up as she scented the wind. Shadow nickered, but Tally didn't look at him. Her attention was fixed on something the breeze was bringing her. Sierra lifted her own head and was startled by the scent of a horse—one horse—that she didn't know. Then it was gone, dissolving into the morning breeze.

Shadow neighed once more and Sierra could hear

his urgency. Had he scented the strange horse, too? Tally led off, trotting when she would normally have walked.

All morning long Shadow kept the herd moving faster than usual. He did not limp anymore, but Sierra could tell that his hind leg was still a little stiff. He insisted on the increased pace. When Tally slowed, he nipped gently at the hindmost mares and made them hurry enough to bump into the mares in front of them so that they all had to speed up, until Tally was trotting again.

The pace felt good to Sierra. She hated ambling slowly when it wasn't hot. The foals were all big enough now to keep up, but they wanted to stop and graze. All the horses did. Sierra could sense their confusion. There was no danger that any of them could see or scent.

By evening, they were in country Sierra had never seen before. The wind had scoured away the soil, uncovering layers of red rock that curved along the hillsides. Tally found a spring and the herd settled in for the night on a broad, low ridge not far

from the water. Fern and Sierra stood close together, dozing standing up through the night.

Only a few of the mares lay down to sleep. Sierra
thought they were foolish. The time it took to
scramble upright to gallop could be the difference
between living and dying in a strange place.

Waking earlier than most of the others, Sierra
stretched and stepped away from Fern to shake herself. She felt her usual dawn restlessness rising, but
knew she shouldn't gallop even a short circle this
early. Few would have slept soundly in this strange
place. Hoofbeats would startle the whole herd into
thinking there was danger near.

Sierra stretched again, then looked downslope
toward the spring. The sun wasn't up yet and the
dawn-dusk was still thick. But she could see a form
standing beside the water and she knew instantly
what it was.

The strange bay stallion had followed them.

Sierra felt her heart sink. Shadow was getting
old. His injured back leg still made him limp sometimes. And this young stallion wanted a herd of his

own, of course. The only way he could have this one was to fight Shadow and win.

As the sun came up, sending a wash of gold and pink across the prairie, the strange stallion's blood-bay coat seemed to dance with the fiery light. *Fire. Fuego.* Sierra tossed her head uneasily. Fire was dangerous. It destroyed everything it touched.

Fuego arched his neck. Sierra watched sadly. He was staring at the herd, his head up, his ears jutted forward.

Sierra nudged Fern, who woke, startled into fear, her eyes rimmed in white. Sierra lowered her own head to show Fern that there was no reason to run. Then she turned to face the spring. Fern followed her gesture and Sierra heard her pull in an abrupt breath.

A few seconds later, Shadow whinnied. It was not an ordinary whinny: it was a challenge. Sierra had only heard the trumpeting call a few times in her life—and not for a long time—but she knew it instantly.

The herd wakened all at once. Mares with foals

called them close. The young stallions trembled with excitement and Sierra watched them line up side by side, their necks arched and their eyes wide. They would all play out this scene themselves, one day.

Shadow came forward, lifting his forelegs high, stopping to rear, then to strike at the air before him. Instead of waiting for Fuego to come up the slope, he plunged down it, his ears flattened against his neck, his tail slicing at the air.

Fuego stood his ground.

Sierra moved forward with the rest of the herd to form a loose line along the curve of the ridge. They all stood, nervous and unhappy—and watching intently.

Shadow broke from a gallop back into a trot when it was clear that Fuego wasn't going to be chased off without a real fight. Sierra watched the older stallion slow, then stand, facing Fuego. An instant later, they were sidestepping, crossing their front legs as they circled each other, their rasping challenges echoing in the still morning.

Shadow struck out again with his forehooves, beating at the air. Fuego reared in response, then pawed, jabbing at the earth, flipping chunks of grass skyward. For another long, terrible moment, both stallions stood far apart, squealing and striking. Then they lunged toward each other.

Sierra flinched at the heavy sound when they came together, teeth bared. Shadow tore at Fuego's shoulder, bringing a welter of blood to his skin. Fuego countered by whirling to face away, kicking upward with both back hooves. Shadow staggered back, off balance long enough for Fuego to whirl and leap at him, biting at his neck.

Sierra stood watching with the others. Not one of them thought that Shadow would win, she was sure. He was smaller and much older. And Fuego's attack was savage. Every horse there knew that this was the way of their world. Young stallions took herds from aging ones. But Shadow had been good to them and it hurt to watch.

When Shadow finally gave up and turned away, limping and breathing hard, Fuego chased him, driving him into a stiff-legged, lurching gallop.

Every horse in the herd was trembling. The horses all stared, knowing they would probably never see Shadow again.

Fuego galloped back and faced them, his sides heaving, his neck arched proudly. Then he threw his head up and trumpeted again. This time it was a cry of victory.

Chapter Five

The weather turned not long after Fuego defeated Shadow. The nights got cooler. Fuego wasted no time. He began by chasing Paco out of the herd. It was awful, but none of us dared challenge him. Then, one by one, he attacked the young stallions and they were forced to leave, condemned to a winter of dangerous solitude unless they could find a band of others like themselves. Shadow would have waited for them to leave on their own in the spring. Then, if any had wanted to fight, he would have faced them bravely. One morning, I saw three of them grazing at a distance and

Shadow was with them. I was so glad to know he wasn't alone. After a moment I made out a smaller shape. Paco had found his old friends as well.

Fuego was always moving restlessly before Sierra opened her eyes. It was strange—all her life she had been the first in the herd to awaken.

The first time Sierra tried to canter in the cold dawn air, Fuego rushed at her, his head low, his neck outstretched like a striking snake. He bit her, *hard*, and she squealed and ran for the safety of the herd.

Blue-gray clouds rolled in and for a few days it seemed as though winter had caught them on the open plains. The wind howled and Sierra stood between her mother and Fern, her head low, her back to the wind.

For three long days, the wind whistled and gusted and there was nothing the horses could do besides bunch close together in the little gully Tally had found for them, trying to stay warm. Their coats had not yet thickened for winter and they all shuddered and shook with cold.

The storm brought a dusting of early snow with it and when the wind finally dropped, the horses found that the autumn grass, though still standing, had frozen. They all ate greedily, even though the icy grass gritted between their teeth.

Then, as the day warmed, there was a smell of bruised greenery in the air. The frozen grass was thawing and it wilted into sad clumps. The following evening, the clumps were slimy, rotting.

Sierra knew that Tally was uneasy. And she knew why. They all did. If the winter was going to come early, it was time to start southward, to the canyons where they usually wintered.

But every morning, Fuego was circling them, pawing at the frosty ground, moving them northward, toward the foothills. His teeth bared, he would stalk Tally, forcing her to lead off, then stayed behind her and Bonita until they were all moving north. Only then would he squeal a warning and gallop back to bring up the rear.

Sierra found herself watching Fuego all the time. If he was headed her way, she found some reason to change direction or to stop—whatever it took so that he passed without noticing her.

Fern was so cautious about irritating the bay stallion that she would stop eating and move off if he approached at all. She wasn't the only one. All the mares stayed clear of him if they could.

Sierra saw her own mother move away from Fuego one evening, acting like she was just restless. Bonita walked a little way, then turned and came back when Fuego had moved on. Then she settled in her usual place beside Tally.

Fuego seemed not to notice. He spent his days circling the herd and his nights standing on high points, keeping watch. Did he ever sleep? Every morning when Sierra opened her eyes, he was already awake.

Once the freakish early snowstorm was long gone, the weather turned warmer. Tally led off one morning, ambling at a comfortable pace, angling westward. Fuego nipped the stragglers forward, running the mares into each other, pushing them along.

He tolerated Tally's direction shift until midday when they stopped to drink from a shallow creek. Then he stayed up front with the lead mare until she was headed north again.

The grass got no better as they went. The early snow had frozen the whole prairie, it seemed. Sierra hated the smell of it and pawed away the frost-killed tops to try to find new shoots coming up in the last warm days of the autumn. It was hard.

One morning, Sierra saw a half-grown colt step up to a clump of grass just as Fuego reached toward it. The colt backed up immediately, and Sierra found herself staring at him. The colt's ribs were visible beneath his skin.

Sierra looked at the others, surprised. They were all losing weight. Fern's hipbones looked sharp and her own flanks were hollow. Fuego's insistence that they travel fast on short rations was taking a toll.

Usually, this time of year, they were all fat from a summer of grazing. Tally would be slowly starting them southwest—headed for the sheltering canyons where the rock overhangs protected them from storms and the willows by the creeks offered food when there was none elsewhere.

One morning, Tally started out headed southwest—as she had tried to every morning since the early snowstorm. Fuego charged to the head of the herd and nipped at her. When she refused to obey him and start north, he squealed in rage. She stopped, and he charged at her.

Tally tossed her head, her nerve finally breaking. She wheeled around in a panic and galloped away from the furious stallion. As Fuego chased her, a flash of white caught Sierra's eye and she looked back at the herd.

Bonita was making her way forward through the other horses. She got to Tally's usual place and simply stopped.

Sierra watched her mother—and waited.

All around her, horses were restless, uneasy. A thudding of hooves against the earth passed through the herd and they stamped with impatience and frustration.

Prancing back toward the herd, Tally galloping before him, Fuego saw Bonita. Tally halted and stood, shaking as Fuego approached Bonita. She kept her head low and stepped forward, heading south as Tally had. Sierra pushed her way forward to follow her mother. In seconds, the whole herd was moving.

Fuego snorted and pawed at the ground. He galloped in a tight circle, flaring his tail and mane as he danced to a stop in front of Bonita. Tally had fallen in beside her and she kept walking, her gait stiff. Now, she stubbornly placed herself between Fuego and Bonita, taking her place at the head of the herd.

Fuego snorted and reared, coming down with a lowered head and fierce eyes until Bonita and Tally slowly veered northward. Then he tried to drive them along faster—but they refused to speed up.

They set themselves side by side, and kept walking. They kept their heads up and their eyes on the foothills ahead. Fuego charged toward them, squealing and biting, demanding that they go faster. Bonita stumbled and had to right herself, but then she kept walking. And the whole herd followed behind them.

Fuego danced in a circle, his teeth bared.

It didn't matter.

Bonita and Tally kept going in Fuego's chosen direction—at *their* chosen speed. Fuego finally galloped to the back of the herd and took up his position.

The herd traveled more slowly after that day. Bonita and Tally sometimes just stopped, ignoring Fuego's objections as the horses spread out to graze. So, even though they continued northward, the foothills closer every day, the horses began to put on a little weight and some of the tension eased.

One chilly evening, Sierra reached back to shoo a mosquito from her flank and noticed that her coat was getting heavier. She glanced at Fern, then at one of the young mares who was standing close.

Sierra shook her mane. They were all growing their winter coats. Autumn was nearly over. Winter would be upon them soon. And they were going to be in the foothills when it did—far from their wide, safe canyon.

Chapter Six

*N*one of us could understand why Fuego had decided we should winter in the foothills. It seemed foolish. Wolves roamed there. So did mountain lions. Why go where they lived when our sheltered red-rock canyons were to the southwest?

One morning, it began to snow as they waited for Tally to set off. To the north, the foothills loomed deep blue in the morning light. Sierra felt odd, backward, as though someone had reversed the direction of the sun.

This was the time of year to be heading *away* from the foothills.

Sierra saw the wet flakes sticking to Fern's coat. They were huge and had blurred edges. The air wasn't winter-cold yet. The snowflakes had half melted before reaching the ground.

Sierra could feel the snowflakes melting on her back. They felt like icy rain drops seeping through her coat and chilling her skin.

It tickled at first. Then it became a misery. And still Tally refused to go forward.

Sierra blinked the flakes out of her eyelashes, then dropped her head to rub her cheek against her foreleg. A quiet squeal made her look forward to the head of the herd. Tally was standing in front of Fuego. He had arched his neck and was looking down his muzzle at her. They were disagreeing about what direction to take again.

Sierra watched. The snow was thickening. The flakes came almost straight down in the still air. Sierra shook to rid herself of them, but within seconds, her back was covered again. She stamped a forehoof.

Sierra shook her mane, impatient and tired of the tension in the herd. Wherever he had come from, Fuego didn't know this country like Tally did. The lead mare had guided Shadow's herd for years—and they had all been happier and better fed than they were now.

Sierra stood still, feeling anger rise inside her. Fuego had changed everything. And now he was leading them into a bad wintering place—one where there was little grass and many dangers.

Tally gave in suddenly and began to walk forward.

Bonita joined her and the herd began to move.

Sierra stood still, even when Fern nudged her. Fuego was brave and strong, but he was making them do something foolish. If he would only trust the mares the way Shadow had ...

Fern nudged her once more and Sierra looked at her old friend, extending her muzzle in a gesture she knew Fern would understand. Fern lowered her head and started forward without her, trotting a few steps to catch up with the others. She looked back and nickered.

Still, Sierra hesitated.

She looked around as the rest of the herd passed, following Tally and her mother toward the hills. She knew why Tally and Bonita had given in. It made sense.

The first early storm would have started them toward the canyons and they'd have had plenty of time to travel that far.

But now the snow was falling fast and thick. To turn around, to go back across the sage prairie *now*, when winter was so close, was foolish. This late in autumn howling storms could rise fast and last for days.

Hidden from Fuego by the dense flurry of snow, Sierra stood her ground until the last of the horses ahead of her had gone past. She waited until the snow had swallowed most of them up. Then, trembling, she made herself stand a few more seconds.

The snowfall was so thick that it muffled sound as well as sight. For an instant, Sierra imagined herself completely alone. It terrified her.

She started forward.

Fuego suddenly appeared out of the wall of snow, his ears back in irritation.

Sierra stared at him. After all the trouble he'd had getting the mares to move, he had still thought to gallop back and see if there were any stragglers. And she was glad to see him, even though she knew he would be irritated and would probably drive her back into the herd.

But he didn't.

To Sierra's amazement, Fuego didn't bite at her. He didn't even bare his teeth. Instead, he galloped up to her, then slid to a stop and turned. Then he simply waited until she began to walk again—and kept up when she broke into a trot.

Chapter Seven

*T*hat first snowstorm only lasted three days.
We huddled in the first valley we came to, a
narrow place with steep sides that made us all
uneasy. But there was plenty of willow and for a
time, it was all right there. Fuego was always on
watch....

The valley was so narrow at one end that it
made a good wind shelter. The first few nights they
settled on their sleeping places and the snow got
trampled down in an uneven circle.

Then another storm came. The snow was lighter

than the first one, not nearly as wet. An occasional shake kept it off their backs.

A week later, the next storm was almost pleasant. There was little wind and the snow fell silently for days. One warm day had melted the snow just enough to crust the top of it. It wasn't hard for the horses to break through, but it was strong enough to support the weight of birds and jackrabbits and their tracks soon crisscrossed the drifts.

Sierra's coat got thicker and warmer as the days passed, matting in the constant wet of the snow. The next storm was heavier. At first, some of the mares went to the wider end of the valley every day and pawed for grass. Most stayed with it only until midday, then they gave up and headed for the thick stands of willow along the little creek.

Sierra tried to find grass, too, but what she did manage to uncover was tough and dried and she gave it up with the rest and ate willow all day long, unless wind or weather drove her back to the shelter of the narrow end of the valley. Now that the snow was almost belly deep, she was grateful for the paths they had worn in the snow.

Fuego kept close watch day and night. He often stood on the ridge above the valley, alone and cold.

One frigid night, Sierra woke to a low snarling sound. She was instantly alert, her eyes wide. There was a big winter moon lighting the snowy earth and she could see Fuego. He was facing something, a shadow the color of rain and earth.

The snarling rose into a sharp, yapping bark and Sierra went rigid. *Wolves.*

Sierra was shaking. How many were there? How close?

A squeal from one of the mares made them all shy and startle. Tally whinnied a warning and they all understood her perfectly.

Gather together. Don't run. If they catch you alone, they will kill you.

Sierra forced herself to walk forward, pressing close to the other mares. She turned so that she was facing outward, her back protected by friends, her teeth and sharp front hooves toward whatever danger might come.

Mares with foals were easing their way toward the center of the loose circle. The colts looked terrified, their eyes big and edged in white.

Fuego screamed suddenly and the horses went still. Sierra looked up at the ridge and tried to make out what was happening.

There were three wolves that she could see. They were circling Fuego, trying to get behind him so they could lame him with a sudden bite.

The mares were trembling, close to panic. Tally whinnied another warning. Bonita made a low sound that Sierra remembered well from her early days. It was the sound a mare makes to reassure her foal and it was instantly echoed throughout the herd. Tally and Bonita circled the mares, pushing them closer together. Then they found places for themselves and faced outward.

Above them, Fuego was locked in a deadly battle. He spun and kicked and Sierra heard one wolf shriek in pain. It scrambled away into the woods.

Fuego plunged in a circle, striking out with his forehooves. A snarling growl chilled Sierra's heart.

But if it scared Fuego, he reacted by wrenching around again, this time kicking so hard that one of the wolves was lifted off its paws and thrown down into the valley. It landed not far from Sierra. It was hurt, she could tell that much. But it was not dead. Without thinking, she charged forward and reared above the wolf. An instant later her mother was beside her, then Tally. Together they ended the wolf's life, translating their fear into an attack.

Up on the ridge, Fuego was squaring off with the last wolf. It snarled and sprang forward, then faded backward to avoid Fuego's hooves. Then it turned and ran. Fuego's hooves stopped pounding. Then there was only the sound of his labored breathing.

The silence went on for so long that Sierra, exhausted and finally feeling safe, dozed off. Fern pressed against her side, keeping her warm. They were all still in a tight circle when Sierra woke the next morning.

Snow was falling. It had almost covered the body of the wolf and the trampled snow around it. Sierra could not look at it without feeling unsteady, so she half turned and looked up on the ridge. Fuego was still there, his head high and his ears stiffly forward as he listened for danger.

Shaking herself, Sierra saw that her mother and Tally were both awake and alert. Bonita whickered, jutting her muzzle upward in the direction of the dead wolf.

Sierra understood the praise, but wondered how she had managed to attack a wolf, even one that was hurt. This morning, in the gray light of dawn, the very scent of its body terrified her. All she wanted was to get away from it.

Glancing at her mother, she stepped out of the circle. Tally made no move to correct her, nor did Fuego, watching from the ridge.

Sierra led the way up the path they had worn in the snow from the narrowest end of the little valley to where it widened along the frozen creek. Fern and most of the others followed her and fell to eating, standing with their heads and shoulders inside the willow thickets. But they were not at ease. Every few seconds each mare jerked her head up to listen. Scent was no help this morning. Their whole valley reeked of wolves.

Sierra walked a little way past them, wading through the snow beyond the end of the path. She found a good place to forage and worked her way closer, careful to set her hooves solidly on the slippery ground.

Shivering, Sierra leaned forward and nibbled at the willow trunk delicately, working at the bark until she could wrinkle it, then pinching the wrinkle between her teeth. She pulled at it in little jerks, peeling off a long strip.

Shuddering at the bitter taste of the bark, Sierra gathered the strip into her mouth a little at a time, chewing steadily.

When she had swallowed the last of it, she worked at the slender trunk again, starting another long, slippery strip of bark. But she couldn't keep herself from glancing up the steep valley walls every few seconds. Were there more wolves out there? Were they close? They would be silent in the snow.

The next morning it was clear. The sun shone,

silvering the snow into a glittering lake of white-ness. The walls of the valley pressed in on Sierra again, and after she had eaten some willow, she left the herd to stand a little way off.

By noon the sky had clouded over and Sierra could smell snow, the sharp, high-pitched odor of a coming storm. She blew out a long breath and shook herself. She hated being in the narrow valley, unable to see, unable to run when danger came.

Fuego came back down into the valley to feed in the afternoon and Sierra touched him with her muzzle when he passed, thanking him for protecting them. He touched her shoulder and Sierra realized that somehow in the night, she had stopped hating him.

As the snow began to fall, Sierra moved away from the others, but stayed within sight. She stood still for a time, then allowed herself to climb the slope.

A light wind was blowing and Sierra drew in a long breath, cleaned of the wolf's scent. She breathed again, more slowly. It *was* clean. There were no wolves, not on this side of the valley rim anyway. And Fuego was close, just below.

Sierra climbed a little higher, wading through the deep snow. She felt something like her old restlessness, but it was different. She didn't want to gallop for joy. She just longed to stand where she could see a horizon.

Letting her urgency take over, Sierra floundered her way upward, then just over the rim of the valley.

She turned and looked back down and was surprised to see how close the herd really was. She moved back from the edge to keep Fuego from seeing her if he looked her way.

The wind was getting stronger. Sierra shivered and walked a little farther, into the shelter of some pine trees.

The clean scent of the wind lulled her and she stared off at the horizon, feeling a weight leave her heart. She hated the valley, hated feeling trapped inside it.

After a few minutes, Sierra approached the rim of the valley again and peeked downward. None of the horses had missed her. They were all intent on filling their bellies. Even Fuego had begun to eat.

As the wind rose, Sierra turned back into the pines. She pawed at the deep snow and was surprised to find a little grass. She turned and pawed again, finding another clump. After the bitter willow bark they had been living on, even dry, frozen grass tasted wonderful.

Eating eagerly, with her head down, Sierra heard a low growl. She jerked upright and whirled, glimpsing amber eyes, catching the terrifying scent of the wolf. Then she sprang into a desperate gallop.

Chapter Eight

I ran until I could go no further. The snow was deep, dragging at my legs and belly. The wind rose to a scream and blew the loose drifts into a stinging mist. I was nearly staggering with effort when I turned to fight. But by then, there was only wind, only snow slanting sharply to the ground. The wolf had gone—or it had never chased me at all. And then I realized I had no idea which way to go.

Sierra tried to find her way back to the valley. She walked for hours, fighting the fierce wind, straining to scent the rushing air. Every whipping branch startled her, every shadow looked, for an instant, like a skulking wolf.

When dusk came, she dozed fitfully in a thick stand of pine trees. Every time she woke she thought she could hear and smell wolf-scent and stood wide-eyed and trembling for a long time before she could get back to sleep. That single night seemed as long as a whole winter should have been.

Clouds hid the moon.

The wind tore at the trees.

The snow was like sand, stinging her eyes shut, sifting through her coat to chafe at her skin.

Morning came, but the wind had not dropped. It felt so strange, so *wrong*, to be alone. Sierra left the pines, afraid to go on, but more afraid to stop. She made her way through the deep snow slowly, guessing at the direction of the little valley. She found a downslope and walked along it, but there were no horses below, no creek, no willow stands. That night she slept fitfully again, sheltered by another stand of pine trees. Through the long darkness she listened to the buffeting roar of the wind.

The next day, Sierra had to stop looking for the

valley in order to seek food. She was getting weak and it scared her. The wind was still high, so she followed the slope of the land downward until the wind mostly passed above her. Then she pawed at the deep snow, feeling for clumps of grass.

She found nothing but rocks.

Going lower still, Sierra hoped to come across a creek. Willow almost always grew along creeks. But the slope opened up and she could only keep going—and when she finally came to the bottom, there was no stream.

That night, Sierra lay down. She knew it was foolish, that if the wolves found her, she would never rise to stand again. But her strength was ebbing. She was hungry—hungrier than she had ever been in her entire life. And she was cold. So cold.

Dawn came long before Sierra opened her eyes. When she did, it took her a moment to remember everything that had happened. It took another moment for her to realize that the wind had finally stopped.

Shaking, she got to her feet. Snow cascaded from her back, landing in soft thuds. She stood still for a long moment, blinking, wishing she knew what to do, where to go.

The snow had drifted and blown during the night. It was a solid white covering laid over the earth, without a single track of any kind marring the windswept surface.

Sierra desolately looked one direction, then another. She knew only one thing for certain—that she would die of cold and hunger if she didn't find food soon. She forced herself to start off.

Along the edge of a stand of pines, she pawed at the snow. Breathing hard, swaying on her feet, she kept at it until she had worked her way to the bottom of the drift. But there was no grass—only a rust-red mat of wet pine needles.

Sierra began walking again. She had to lift each hoof high, stepping over the surface of the deep snow, wearily plowing her way forward. She listened for a low snarl with every step. Wolves knew that horses were nearly helpless in deep snow. And Sierra knew she would be an easier target than most, as weak as she was.

By nightfall she had found only two clumps of

grass, but she ate every wisp eagerly and she felt a little better as the darkness settled into the pines around her.

Then, as the night went on, her loneliness enclosed her and she began to tremble. She had never been alone for so long in her life. At least her belly had a little grass in it, she told herself. Maybe she would be strong enough to find the herd soon. There was no scent of horses in the clean, sharp air. But maybe the breeze would bring news of them.

The next morning, Sierra woke with a small flame of hope in her heart. But by midday it was fading. There was no grass where she was. Only rocks and pine needles and buried thickets of ill-smelling bushes that she knew to be poison. And there was still no scent of the herd.

Wandering slowly and almost aimlessly, she stumbled into a creek bottom and gratefully took a long drink of icy water. But there was no willow, and as night closed in again she could not climb the slope to find a safer place to sleep. She was too weak. She fell asleep aching for the warmth of her mother, her friends. She even wished that Fuego were nearby, watching for danger while she rested.

The following morning, Sierra woke with a start. There were strange, sharp sounds, calls that were foreign to her ears.

Then she caught a glimpse of something through the trees and even though she had only heard them a few times in her life, she recognized the sound.

Human voices.

They echoed and bounded across the slope, then back.

Sierra struggled upright and stood, swaying, staring out at the flat ground where the creek wound, then at the slopes above, trying to figure out which direction the sounds were coming from.

There were hoofbeats, too, she realized, horses galloping faster than was safe in this deep snow. What were they running from? The human beings?

Sierra listened. The human cries were sharp, like thorns, like a striking hoof; they reminded her of the rending squeals that stallions made in battle.

Stumbling, falling, then scrambling upright again,

Sierra made her way desperately up the slope toward the pines. She managed to stagger in among the trees just as the sound of hooves changed direction and the muted thunder of galloping horses came toward her.

Sierra stood trembling, watching, as a herd of horses thundered into the clearing. Men mounted on horses rode hard behind them, chasing them, driving them forward. The humans kept glancing anxiously behind themselves, watching for something. It was as though they had stolen the horses. But from where?

Sierra stared. She had seen horses with humans on their backs before—but never this close. These humans had long dark manes and smelled of smoke. They were screeching, and some lashed at their horses with what looked like long vines.

Suddenly, another group of humans rode into the valley, shouting and screaming furiously at the first group. They all forced their horses to gallop even faster through the dangerously deep snow.

It was horrifying. It looked painful and she wondered how the horses stood it. Lions rode horses in the death hunt, wolves would sometimes leap onto a horse's back, especially when deep snow made it easier. But these humans were not trying to kill the horses beneath them.

They were trying to kill each other.

Crying out, letting the free horses gallop on alone, they pulled their mounts around in arcs, then beat at each other with long sticks as they passed. Two of them fell into the snow and did not rise. Their horses galloped on, the long vines trailing from their necks. One of these horses was a tall black-and-white pinto that raced along, swift and sure, leaping another fallen human to avoid trampling it, then disappearing into the trees across the valley.

Sierra could only watch, astounded as the fight went on. Then, suddenly, the horses split into two groups and galloped away. The humans were still shouting, one group of riders driving the free horses ahead of them.

A heavy silence settled over the clearing and

Sierra let out a long breath. They had not seen her. She was safe. She shook her mane weakly. Safe?

She was safe to continue starving to death. Or freezing to death. Or both ... while she waited for wolves to come.

Sierra lowered her head and fought the desire to just lie down again. She knew she needed to find food. She would never find the herd unless she could travel. But how? She licked at the snow, letting it wet her mouth, then tried to lift her head, tried to make herself begin pawing at the snow again. But she just couldn't find the strength. She longed for Fern's company. Fern and her mother would have cleared the snow away for her.

She looked up at the sky. Clouds were piling up. Was it going to storm?

The sudden sound of hooves made her turn her head.

Had the humans come back?

She tried to flounder forward, deeper into the pines.

But it was only a single horse, the tall black-and-white pinto. His coat was dusted with snow now from walking through the pines.

As Sierra stared at him, his markings shifted with his stride, like storm clouds. He was dragging one long vine from his neck. He passed into the bluish shadow of a pine tree on a little ridge and for a moment he blended with the cloudy sky, part of the storm that was approaching.

Storm whinnied softly. Sierra continued to stare, not quite sure he was real, afraid of the long vine dangling from his neck, the smell of people still in the air. He whinnied again. It took Sierra a long moment to realize that he was whinnying at *her*.

Chapter Nine

*T*he first time I saw him, Storm seemed almost as lost as I was. After the first days of our time in the forest, I had much to teach him. But without him, I would have died in those snowy woods. I have never doubted that, not for an instant. I was so hungry, so afraid, so alone. I was close to giving up before he found me. I owe Storm my life.

Sierra lifted her head a little and tried to answer. Her own voice sounded weak and uncertain. Storm whinnied again, and there was concern in his tone.

Sierra closed her eyes, swept by a feeling of relief.

She was no longer alone.

That single fact changed everything.

Storm neighed, tossing his head. He shook his mane and then broke into a canter. He came toward her as fast as he could, floundering in the deep snow until he had to break back into a trot, then a walk where the slope steepened.

He came closer, an eager, happy light in his eyes, his ears pricked forward. Sierra realized he was as glad to see her as she was to see him.

But his friendly, warm breath on her face—and the strange scents that surrounded him—made Sierra back up a step.

He instantly stopped, then backed up himself, like a colt who has been reminded of his manners. He stood quietly, waiting for Sierra to let him know he could approach her.

Sierra blinked, each cold breath bringing her scents she did not know, did not want to know. Among them was smoke, which meant Storm had been near fire.

Fire!

What kind of horse remained near fire?

Sierra had smelled smoke mixed with human scent before. She had hidden with the herd as human beings passed across the prairie with their awkward two-legged strides. She hadn't known what the fire scent meant then and she didn't know now. Fire swept the land and killed horses and jackrabbits and mice and wolves and every other living thing it could catch.

Didn't it kill humans?

Didn't it kill the horses who lived with them?

Storm shook his head and the vine thing hanging down from his neck jerked back and forth in the air. He didn't seem to notice. Sierra blinked and ducked her head.

Sierra stared at Storm. The vine wrapped around his neck and dangled from his jaw. It smelled horrible, like rotting flesh and humans and smoke. She lifted her head to avoid some of the scent.

Storm edged toward her, taking the gesture as permission to come closer. Sierra backed away once again, her breath catching at the smells.

Storm's ears drooped and she knew she had offended him, but didn't know what to do about it. The ache in her stomach—hunger and fear—suddenly seemed less important to her than avoiding the awful smells.

As though he understood, Storm turned slowly and started down the slope. Sierra's heart caught. Was he leaving her? Then, after a few strides, he turned and looked back at her.

It was an invitation so like any of the herd might have given her that Sierra leaned forward and took a single step without hesitating. Then she kept going because she was afraid he would leave her alone.

Walking was easier when another horse broke a path through the snow. The unfamiliar and scary scents that drifted back to Sierra kept her alert and uneasy, but they did not keep her from following Storm as he led her resolutely downward, then along the creek at the bottom of the slope.

Sierra walked, stiff-legged and slow, and sometimes he had to wait for her to catch up. Over and over he stood patiently while she made her way toward him, then started again, more slowly.

Sierra was nearly at the end of her strength more than once, but each time she found some way to keep going. The sun passed overhead as they slowly moved through the deep snow. Her hunger ached and cramped at her belly and she was thirsty again. Storm waited as she made her way close to the creek, then bent to drink.

Most of the afternoon was gone before they rounded a bend in the creek and came out of a stand of cottonwoods—and Sierra's heart leaped at the sight of willow thickets. The slender gold-brown branches crowded the banks of the creek so densely that it was impossible to see where they ended.

Storm walked steadily until they reached the willow, then, incredibly, he kept walking.

Sierra stopped and began the nibbling and scraping it took to free a strip of bark. She closed her eyes, frantic to fill her belly, not even noticing the bitter taste of the bark.

A low whickering made her look. Storm was a few strides away, facing her. He had turned and come back along his own tracks. His ears were up and he was staring at her.

Sierra did not stop chewing. She could not.

Storm whickered again.

Sierra lifted her head and shook her mane, then she tore another strip of willow bark free. Chewing it, staring at Storm, she was certain of only one thing: nothing could make her leave this willow thicket before her belly was full. Nothing.

Storm heaved out a long breath. He rubbed his muzzle on his foreleg and straightened, then looked at the slope above them.

Sierra ripped another piece of bark loose and began to eat it, her jaw working furiously, automatically.

Storm glanced upward again and Sierra followed his gaze. It was getting late in the day. It would be dusk before much longer. She ate faster, tearing at the bark.

They found a place among some pines that

seemed safe enough. Sierra had to nudge Storm farther into the trees than he wanted to go. Now that she had a belly full of willow bark, and a little of her strength back, she was not about to sleep where wolves might see her. It was wonderful to have Storm's warmth as the night got colder. He made her feel safer than she had since she'd gotten lost. She slept through the night.

The next day, Storm was hungry enough to learn how to eat willow bark. He wrinkled his upper lip, and shuddered. Sierra switched her tail and sidled, then wrinkled her own to let him know she understood. Willow was bitter. But it would keep them alive.

On the third day, Storm rolled in the snow, wriggling, all four hooves in the air. Sierra took his example, then shook the snow from her coat. He smelled less like smoke after that, and she was glad.

On a cold afternoon, as they stood side by side in the pines, Sierra accidentally stepped on the vine thing that hung down Storm's neck as he grazed on frozen grass he'd uncovered. Startled, he jerked his head and it snapped and dropped to the snow. He didn't seem to mind losing it, though he sniffed at it for a moment before they moved on down the slope. Sierra felt a deep sense of relief as they left the human scent behind.

Chapter Ten

*S*torm would not stay in the valley near the willow thickets, so I followed him. Blizzards came and went. Twice we found whole meadows of buried grass that sustained us for days. As spring warmed the land, I began to feel strong again. I knew I might never see the herd again, but I was less afraid. Storm was a good companion, even-tempered and kind. That spring the creeks ran high. I thought that Storm and I would soon begin a new herd, would bring foals into the wide lands he led me across that summer. But he never stopped moving. I didn't understand why for a long time.

One morning, Sierra woke to a faint smell of smoke in the air. Frightened, she nudged Storm awake. The stallion nudged her back, pressing his forehead against her neck as he often did. Then he opened his eyes and yawned. But the scent of smoke was very faint and he seemed not to notice it.

This was not the first time that Sierra had noticed something long before Storm did. Usually it didn't matter, but this time she wanted him to be as worried as she was. But if he smelled the smoke, he didn't seem bothered by it at all. Sierra led him away from it, grazing as they went, heading northward through the foothills until it was gone and the air was clean again.

As spring burst into bloom, Sierra grew sleek. She began to gallop for joy in the mornings again. Storm did not mind. He often joined her. Sierra loved him for it. The old restlessness would rise and Storm would race after her and she would slow to let him catch up. They splashed through the cold river shallows and pounded across the meadows together, sometimes startling the deer that drank silently in the early mist by the river. The days were warm and wonderful and Sierra woke every morning at dawn and realized with joy that Storm was beside her.

Then, the smell of smoke came again. This time it was much stronger. Sierra could smell scorching flesh, too. A wildfire? This time of year when the grass was low and green? It made no sense.

This time Storm noticed the scent. He turned to face the wind and inhaled deeply. Sierra stood close to him and waited for him to turn away from the horrible stench. But he didn't. He set off walking *toward* it.

Sierra hung back. Storm stopped. He whinnied at her and there was an urgency in his tone. Sierra shook her mane and stamped a forehoof. He stared at her, obviously puzzled by her nervousness.

For a long time they looked at each other, then Storm turned and set off again. This time, Sierra looked at the broad lonely expanse of the forest behind her. Then she started after him. The scent of smoke got no stronger as they traveled and sometimes it was gone altogether. Sierra tried not to worry about it. Storm had never done anything to hurt or scare her. He wouldn't now.

At that moment, Sierra felt something deep inside herself. It was odd, tickly, like nothing she had ever felt before. And she knew instantly what it was. She was carrying Storm's foal inside her belly. She looked at him, walking solidly in front of her, his ears up, more and more alert as the days passed. But she longed to have other mares to stand close by—a herd—to be protective of her now.

Sierra promised herself that her foal would be one of the few to make it through a winter. They would find a good sheltered place close to willow thickets and Storm would stop his traveling at last. He would stay with her and he would help wear paths in the snow next winter. They would be all right. They had to be.

Then, a few days later, close to dusk, they came over a ridge and Sierra stopped in her tracks to stare. There, below them, was a sight Sierra could barely believe. There was a mass of tall glowing shapes unlike anything she had ever seen—like gigantic flowers, turned stem up and set upon the ground, glowing like flickering yellow moons.

Storm nudged at her shoulder, then began to pick his way down the slope. Sierra stood helplessly as he walked away from her, heading toward the strange glow.

She flinched when the wind changed and brought her the scent of fire and humans. She could see humans coming out of openings in the glowing amber shapes. The glow was the color of fire, she realized. Humans often smelled of fire. These were their caves then? Shelters?

Then, when a human voice called out, Sierra stepped backward, trembling.

Storm didn't stop. He walked closer and closer. Then he stood still as one of the humans came close enough to encircle his neck. A smaller human stood back a little at first, then came forward, its gait off-rhythm and awkward.

Sierra shuddered as Storm went with them, disappearing into the herd of humans and their odd shelters. She dropped her head, her muzzle nearly touching the ground. He whinnied, looking back over his shoulder. She answered, but then he passed out of her sight.

Sierra stayed awake all night, frantic and lonely again. She waited anxiously, hoping that Storm would soon escape and come back to her. She agonized about going to help him, to try to find him, but her fear of the humans kept her still, hidden in the pines.

In the first pale light of dawn, she risked a little time to go graze; she would need her strength if they had to gallop to get away. But he did not come. Then she heard him whinny and she answered him. He called to her over and over and she answered. But still, he did not come.

The day passed slowly and Sierra stared for hours at the humans' shelters. She could see humans walking back and forth, could hear them talking. The shelters looked less like flowers in the daylight. Each one had a splayed thicket of slim logs jutting out of the top.

The next morning, just before dawn, Sierra forced herself down the slope, her head high, scenting the wind. The humans were silent, still sleeping. Out of the tangle of scents that rose from their shelters, Sierra finally found the one she hoped to find. Storm!

She whinnied. It was a long, aching sound, and it had her heart in it.

Storm answered. She couldn't see him, but she whinnied again, hoping wildly that he would come galloping out to meet her and they could escape this awful place.

Sierra whinnied again and Storm answered, his neighing as urgent as her own.

Then human voices startled Sierra into whirling around and galloping halfway up the slope. When she looked back she saw the little human with the awkward gait standing in the meadow below.

The next day, Sierra grazed early, then stood watching. Just at dawn Storm appeared with the lame-gaited little human following him. Terrified, but determined to get close enough to help her mate,

Sierra galloped straight down the hill.

Storm whinnied a joyous greeting. Then he turned and nuzzled the little human.

Sierra slid to a stop, rearing, then circling. Every muscle in her body was tense. She was ready to explode into a gallop, ready to defend herself and Storm. But he only stood with his neck arched, looking at her, his eyes bright. The little human was rubbing his shoulder now and making small sounds. Then she moved back, keeping hold of the vine that circled Storm's neck.

Sierra shook her mane and came forward, drawn to Storm so strongly that her fear was pushed aside. He was her mate. He had saved her life. And she had no herd, no other friend here.

Storm whickered and they touched muzzles, exchanging breath. He smelled of humans again, and of smoke, but he also smelled of himself. Sierra fought her impulse to gallop away. Her great need to stay beside Storm won out.

She looked past him. The human was a colt, she realized. It was young. And it had been hurt badly, somehow. One of its legs was bent and weak. Sierra stared, wondering where the human mother was. This colt would need extra care. It could never run from wolves. But there was no mother close by.

For the rest of the summer, Sierra visited Storm when the human colt brought him into the meadow. Storm seemed to have no desire to leave the humans. Still, Sierra was shocked the first time she saw a human riding him. It wasn't the colt-human, but a much bigger one, with squared shoulders and big feet. Sierra followed for a ways, then stopped, heartbroken, when the humans guided the horses out onto an open plain. How could she follow without being seen?

It was nearly dark when Storm and the other horses returned. Sierra stayed hidden but her heart soared. The next time Storm left, she wasn't as scared. By the time the nights were getting chilly, she worried only a little.

Big-Shoulders and Little-Colt were brother and sister. That much became clear as time went on. They smelled almost alike, and they stood close.

They touched each other with trust and ease. And they played sometimes, Big-Shoulders swinging Little-Colt in circles. He looked strong—and could easily have hurt Little-Colt when they played. But it was clear as rainwater that he loved her.

And Storm loved them both.

As impossible as it seemed to Sierra, it was true. His bond with them was like hers with Fern. He *trusted* them. Sierra began to look at the humans a little differently. Were they worthy of trust?

Little-Colt brought Storm to the meadow nearly every day. Once in a while the older human would come with her. His voice was deep and calm. Little-Colt's voice was high, like birdsong.

One morning, Big-Shoulders brought another coiled vine. He spoke softly, and took a step toward Sierra. Little-Colt ran to stand in front of him. Sierra cantered away, then stood watching from the shelter of the pines as they faced off. Amazingly, Little-Colt won the disagreement. Big-Shoulders left.

Later that day, Little-Colt brought corn in a basket. Sierra had never seen such odd food. But

Storm's eagerness encouraged her. Little-Colt stepped back. Sierra came forward and put her muzzle in the basket alongside Storm's. The corn was delicious. It was—incredible! She lifted her muzzle and wrinkled her upper lip to smell the sweet corn scent undiluted by the human scent of the basket.

Little-Colt suddenly curved her mouth, baring her teeth, then made a choppy, odd, high-pitched sound that startled Sierra into backing up.

Instantly, Little-Colt covered her mouth with one hand. She moved her eyes to keep from staring. She turned her body just a little so that Sierra understood that she would not suddenly lunge at her, that she meant no harm. Sierra blinked. These were kind gestures. Little-Colt's manners were very good.

Reassured, Sierra cautiously stepped back toward the basket. Storm had nearly finished, but she managed to steal a little of the corn from him. He rested his muzzle against her neck as she finished. Then, for a long time, they just stood together, enjoying the late-summer day.

Little-Colt stood back. She was still and silent

and Sierra nearly forgot that she was there.

Little-Colt brought the basket nearly every day as the summer passed. She stood a little closer each day and Sierra felt less wary as time went on. By the time the weather was cooling off and autumn was close, Sierra was beginning to trust her.

One day Little-Colt touched her neck. Sierra trembled, but kept eating from the basket. She felt a tug on her mane and when she shook her head, she saw that a strand of the white hair was now the color of a meadow flower.

Little-Colt held a small, cupped basket and a willow stick. Its end was frayed. Sierra sniffed at it. Did Little-Colt eat willow, too? Why would she now, when there was good grass?

Little-Colt showed her the bowl next. Sierra breathed in its smell slowly and carefully, hoping it held something good to eat. Instead, it was full of something that smelled like mud, but was the color of flowers. Little-Colt dipped the frayed willow stick into the mud. Then she leaned forward, talking quietly.

She touched the stick to Sierra's hip, drawing it

lightly across her coat, twice. Then she stood back. Sierra turned to see the bright marks. She quivered her skin. The brightly colored mud didn't hurt. It felt cool as it seeped through to her skin.

Little-Colt made a soft, strange sound—the one she made when Big-Shoulders played with her. Sierra shook her mane again. Whatever it was, the flower-colored mud seemed to make Little-Colt happy. She went back to eating her corn.

As the weather cooled and the nights got cold, Sierra heard wolves howling during the full moon. Uneasy, she began sleeping closer to the humans.

The weather held for a while, chilly nights with sunny days. Now, when Little-Colt brought corn, Storm barely got his share. As all mares do, Sierra knew where her hunger was coming from. It was the foal inside her, growing big, preparing to leave her body.

Chapter Eleven

*T*ime passed, and Little-Colt was good to
me. As my foal kicked and grew inside me,
she brought me corn and cut-grass and other
gifts. Twice I almost touched her. I knew Storm
would like us to be friends, but the old fear
would not let me come that close to her.

The weather was turning cold and Sierra knew
that winter was not too far off. And she finally had
to stop ignoring the uneasiness that was blooming
deep in her heart.

This *was* the wrong time of year to be having a
colt. The sheltered place she had imagined, with a

creek and willow thickets, was impossible now.

Without the protection of a herd, with Storm sleeping with the human herd at night, how would she keep the foal safe? For the thousandth time she longed to somehow make Storm leave this place, but she knew that he would not.

She shook her mane. It was not so bad here. Little-Colt was kind and the corn she brought had been good for Sierra's foal, she was sure.

One day when Sierra was standing quietly with Storm in the meadow, she looked up to see several humans—all of them with big shoulders and big feet—staring at her.

Storm did not seem afraid, so, trembling, Sierra stood still. But then she noticed that they carried the long trailing vines, coiled up like snakes over their arms.

Stepping back, her fear rising, Sierra glanced toward the pine trees at the top of the ridge. Her breath caught. Were there humans up there, too? There were! How had she been so careless? Why hadn't she heard them?

Little-Colt made a sound, then called out something to the other humans.

The ones upslope started walking toward Sierra, quietly, all of them looking aside, at the sky, at each other, but never directly at her. Sierra was not fooled. She reared and leaped away, startling Storm into galloping with her.

They did not get far.

From all sides, humans appeared, scattered in long lines, each one carrying a vine-snake.

Shouts broke out—and a high-pitched wailing that Sierra recognized as Little-Colt's voice. She glanced back to see the small human running after her and Storm, her gait lopsided, but swifter than the big-shouldered humans nonetheless.

Forced to a standstill by the humans closing in from all four sides, Sierra stood shaking, Storm standing close beside her. Even he was uneasy now.

Little-Colt reached the first line of humans and ran between them, then turned and faced them. She lowered her head and kept her eyes on the ground. But she began to make sounds, and Sierra could see the humans were listening.

Sierra's fear raged inside her. She had to protect herself, the foal inside her, but how?

Then, a deeper human voice began making sounds and Little-Colt fell silent.

Sierra looked up to see Big-Shoulders hurrying toward them. Behind him was a human that Sierra had never seen before, another broad-shouldered one. His voice was low and the moment he began making sounds, all the others fell silent. He was tall and heavily built. And he had the longest mane Sierra had ever seen. It was black, streaked with silver.

Long-Mane came into the circle. He held up one hand and began to make the sounds again. He went on for a long time. Twice he gestured at Little-Colt. Sierra could see Little-Colt stand taller each time.

Twice he gestured toward Storm, then toward Big-Shoulders, then back at Little-Colt. Then he did something that Sierra would never forget. He walked toward her, his step so quick, so sure, that she could not move. He laid one hand on Sierra's forehead, lightly, gently, then turned away.

Sierra stood very still. He smelled like Big-Shoulders, like Little-Colt—but he was much older. Sierra understood. He was their father.

Long-Mane gestured toward her again as he faced the ring of humans. He pointed at his own chest, then at Little-Colt once more. Then he walked away.

The humans who had meant to capture Sierra made noises, quiet ones, as they followed Long-Mane back toward their shelters. Little-Colt's mouth was turned up and Sierra could see the sparkle of her eyes. Big-Shoulders embraced her. And then he walked away, too.

Storm whickered at Little-Colt. She ran to embrace his neck and Sierra backed away, her legs still trembling.

Sierra wasn't sure exactly how humans settled their differences, but she knew that something had been decided once and for all.

Long-Mane was like Shadow, or Fuego. He was a decision-maker, a leader. And she was pretty sure he had decided that the humans would leave her alone—that she could run free.

Little-Colt patted Storm's neck once more, then dropped the end of the vine and walked a little way off. She dropped to the ground in the awkward way of all humans, and turned aside so that Sierra could relax.

Sierra whickered softly, thanking Little-Colt. Little-Colt glanced at her. When their eyes met, Sierra saw what Storm saw in the human colt. She had a good heart. A true heart.

Chapter Twelve

*E*very day after that, Little-Colt brought Storm to visit me. More than once I saw Long-Mane watching her from the edge of the meadow. She did not see him, I don't think. He stood the way a stallion does when he is on watch. He looked ready to protect Little-Colt against anything. But, of course, it was only Storm and me in the meadow, and so there was no need to protect her at all. I got used to seeing the flower-color in my mane and on my hip. When it began to fade, Little-Colt made it bright again.

Sierra settled in a stand of pines that grew just a little upslope from the meadow. She was sure the humans knew where she slept, but she knew she would be able to smell them coming. She had slowly gotten used to the scents of smoke and the food they ate, so she could pick out small changes in the wind-scents.

And the place she had chosen was far enough from their shelters to give her time to escape if they tried to tie her with the long vines. She was sure Long-Mane had told them not to try—but her foal was getting closer—and her instinctive caution was stronger every day.

Each morning was a little bit colder. The grass in the meadow was getting tough and sparse and Sierra began to feel terribly alone when Storm was not with her—and sometimes even when he was.

She longed for Fern, for her mother, for Paco and Shadow—all her old friends. More than anything she longed for a herd to live among. She began to hate the time spent alone, waiting for Little-Colt to bring Storm to graze.

But as uncomfortable and lonely as she sometimes was, Sierra did not consider leaving the meadow for good. Winter was closing in and she had to consider her own safety—and her foal's. But even more than the reasons any horse would have, she did not want to leave Storm—or Little-Colt. She had become fond of the little human. Sierra would help Little-Colt if danger came; she was sure Little-Colt would protect her, too.

As the days passed, the weather got chillier. It began to drizzle rain early in the mornings. Sierra shivered and grazed on the last of the year's green grass, eating eagerly, grazing until dark every day.

Storm could tell about the foal coming, Sierra was sure. Her sides were bulging. He stood closer to her when they grazed. And when Little-Colt led him away in the evenings, he walked slowly and kept looking back at Sierra.

They began to whinny back and forth, as they had at first; Sierra was uneasy when she couldn't see him. But her uneasiness was a vague thing now. The smell of the humans' fires was familiar, and it kept the wolves away. In a way, Sierra knew, these humans had become her herd.

Big-Shoulders walked to the edge of the meadow one morning. As always, he was quiet and stayed far enough away so that Sierra did not have to canter to the other side of the clearing. But he stood behind a tree and it bothered her to have him acting like a wolf on the prowl.

Maybe he thought she couldn't see him?

When he left, Sierra whinnied a farewell to let him know she had not been fooled. He looked back through the branches and bared his teeth in that odd, human way that let her know he understood.

One moonlit morning, Sierra woke up restless. It wasn't the old kind of restlessness that made her want to gallop—it was something different.

She came out of her sheltering pines to stand in the open. Then she walked back. She lay down again. Then she stood up. The feeling that she had to move came upon her again and she obeyed it once more, switching her tail. She paced back down into the meadow, her head high, her breath coming quick.

A rustling sound caught her attention and she saw a pair of small gray shadows coming toward her across the meadow. Their scent came with them so she was not afraid. It was a pair of skunks, waddling busily, staying side by side as they came through the grass.

Like any sensible horse, Sierra moved out of their way. But for some reason, they changed direction and headed straight for her again.

In order to avoid them, Sierra had to move toward the humans' shelters, closer than she had ever been. As the skunks passed, Sierra's whole body was suddenly gripped by a squeezing pain. Startled, she grunted and sank to her knees, then lay down. The foal was coming.

It took a long time.

Sierra was scared, but she knew her mother had borne her. Mares back to the beginning of time had given birth to foals in meadows just like this one. She lowered her head and waited. The squeezing pains came again and again.

Just as dawn broke, Sierra's foal arrived. It was a filly, a fine brown-and-white pinto with a lovely face.

Sierra did her best to keep her foal warm, moving closer to her, scrubbing at her birth-damp coat with her muzzle and her tongue.

Sierra could not stop staring at the tiny filly. It was amazing to touch her, to smell her scent, which was a mixture of her own and Storm's.

The hours passed slowly. Sierra kept scenting the wind for danger, but she knew that the worst of enemies, lions or wolves, were unlikely to come this close to the humans. Maybe that was why Storm had brought them here … that and his affection for Little-Colt and Big-Shoulders.

The tiny filly was strong. It wasn't long before she struggled upright and took her first wobbling steps. And at that instant, it began to rain.

Rain, Sierra thought.

It was the perfect name.

The soft sound of a human voice startled Sierra. She got up, still exhausted, and saw Little-Colt standing quietly only a few strides away. How long had she been there?

Rain wobbled forward on her long legs, barely keeping her balance.

Little-Colt made a quick, soft sound and Sierra could hear her sigh. Little-Colt met her eyes again, and Sierra saw only kindness there.

The newborn filly lifted her muzzle and licked at her lips, tasting the rain. Then she spotted Little-Colt.

Rain and Little-Colt stared at each other, separated by a step or two, a single breath, no more than that.

Rain started forward.

Sierra nudged her back.

Little-Colt made a tiny sound. Sierra could see the love in her eyes.

Rain started forward a second time. Sierra held still. She watched Rain touch Little-Colt's cheek with her velvety muzzle.

Chapter Thirteen

*T*he day after Rain was born, Long-Mane
and Big-Shoulders came to the meadow.
Long-Mane was leading Storm. Uneasy, I nickered for Rain to stay behind me. But they did
not come close. Long-Mane took the vine from
Storm's neck, then simply stood back....

Storm galloped toward Sierra and Rain. Rain,
startled by the suddenness and the sound of his
hooves, leaped to hide behind her mother. Sierra
stood very still, waiting.

Storm slowed, then stopped, lowering his head.
Rain peeked out. Sierra could feel the tickle of

Rain's breath as she walked in a circle, peering at her father from between Sierra's front legs, from beneath her belly.

A few days later, Big-Shoulders came to the meadow. Storm walked toward him, his head high, his nostrils flared. Sierra held her breath. Big-Shoulders touched Storm, but Storm quickly stepped back. He stood solidly between the humans and Sierra.

Rain danced in a stiff-legged circle. She was just learning to canter. Big-Shoulders curved his mouth upward and watched without trying to come any closer.

The next morning, Big-Shoulders came to the meadow with Little-Colt. They both walked into the open, then stopped, standing quietly. Storm went toward them. Before Sierra could react, Rain galloped to catch up with him, her small hooves pattering on the earth.

While Storm stood quietly for a few seconds, letting his human friends touch him, Rain approached Big-Shoulders. She stopped, then extended her neck and muzzle as far as she could. Big-Shoulders reached out and touched her gently.

Rain did not shy away.

Sierra let out a long breath. Her daughter was not afraid of the humans. Why should she be? She was born here, among these scents. This was her herd. Sierra shook her mane and caught a glimpse of the bright-colored strand. She rarely noticed it or the mark on her hip anymore—they had become familiar, marks of Little-Colt's friendship.

Sierra knew what Tally would think about all this—and Fuego, and Shadow, and Fern. They would think she was foolish to put herself and her foal in danger.

Sierra lifted her head. It didn't matter what they would think. They could not understand. None of them had ever needed friendship and found it in a human heart. But she had. And so had her daughter.

Sierra looked at Little-Colt and Big-Shoulders. They both met her eyes. Their mouths curved upward and she could see the whiteness of their teeth.

Sierra understood and nickered back at them. Rain burst into a stilt-legged canter and galloped a wide circle around them all.